To Sophia

My best Christmas wishes!

Mrs. Claus
2011

Dear Mrs. Claus,
I was wondering if the elves have birthday parties?
Love Katelyn
P.S. Please say Hi to Santa.

Dear Katelyn,

Yes, the elves have birthday parties. It seems like every week someone is having their special day.

Let me tell you about the biggest party of the year. It's not a birthday party, it's a costume party. It's always the 1st of December.

Everyone has so much fun.

And the prizes are so special that it
makes it even more exciting.

First the elves spend all their free time going through books looking for ideas of what to be.

Then they do lots of drawings.

Then they make practice costumes.

OOPS!

It takes almost a month of drawing, of sewing,
and of course trying on their costumes.

Soon all the costumes are done and put away, so we
can plan for the games and prizes.

It is time for me to start baking, and baking, and baking...

Santa likes the baking part.

On the day of the party there are lots
of games to play.

Everyone loves riding the reindeer.

And the elves are really good at building
whole families of snow people.

Here are the elves before they
put on their costumes.

Ryan

Brady

Nicholas

Christina

Chelsea

Mark

Justin

Juan

Do you know who is who?

Let's see if the judges know.

It looks like the judges have guessed who everyone is, except that very tall clown.

No one knows who he or she is. Do you know?

"Please take off your mask.
We can't wait any longer."

"Oh my gosh, it's Chelsea standing
on Christina's shoulders!
That must have been hard to do."

"It was, Mrs. Claus. We almost toppled over
a couple of times."

"You did a fantastic job! Santa will be here in a minute.
He is bringing the prizes."

"Ho Ho Ho! Chelsea and Christina,
I would like to present you with the
first prize ribbon for a job well done."

"This year Mrs. Claus and I are presenting
a very special prize. Are you ready?"
"Yes, Santa what is it?"

"I would like both of you to ride with
me on Christmas Eve."

"Really, Santa?
We get to ride with you on
Christmas Eve?"

"Yipee!
We are going with Santa on Christmas Eve!"

The rest of the evening we danced and sang songs.
We laughed and laughed.

It was so much fun.

Now you know about our special party. I hope you and your family have a wonderful Christmas. Santa says Hi!

Love Mrs. Claus

To Todd and Nicole.
What an amazing journey it was watching and helping
you two grow up.
What incredible adults you have become.
Thank you for all your encouragement.

Mom

Santa's Prize written by Nancy Claus
Copyright ©2006 Nancy Claus
Woodbridge, CA

Published by Cypress Bay Publishing
P.O. Box 984
Woodbridge, CA 95258-0984
www.cypressbaypublishing.com

Text/Story Copyright ©2006 by Nancy Claus
Illustrations Copyright ©2006 Steve Ferchaud
Cover Design: Steve Ferchaud and Tom Watson
Layout, Design, Production: Tom Watson, René Schmidt, www.BookBuilders.net
Publisher: Cypress Bay Publishing

"Santa's Prize" ISBN 0-9746747-5-3
Library of Congress Cataloging-in-Publication Data
Library of Congress Control Number (LCC) 2005906173

Summary: Mrs.Claus answers a letter from a young girl about a wonderful costume party for the elves with a special prize presented by Santa Claus himself.

Additional subjects: Santa Claus, Mrs. Claus, Elves, Costume Parties, Prizes, Holidays, Celebrations

Printed In Hong Kong   First Printing